# A NOTE TO PARENTS

When your children are ready to "step into reading," giving them the right books—and lots of them—is as crucial as giving them the right food to eat. **Step into Reading Books** present exciting stories and information reinforced with lively, colorful illustrations that make learning to read fun, satisfying, and worthwhile. They are priced so that acquiring an entire library of them is affordable. And they are beginning readers with an important difference—they're written on four levels.

**Step 1 Books,** with their very large type and extremely simple vocabulary, have been created for the very youngest readers. **Step 2 Books** are both longer and slightly more difficult. **Step 3 Books,** written to mid-second-grade reading levels, are for the child who has acquired even greater reading skills. **Step 4 Books** offer exciting nonfiction for the increasingly proficient reader.

Children develop at different ages. **Step into Reading Books,** with their four levels of reading, are designed to help children become good—and interested—readers *faster*. The grade levels assigned to the four steps—preschool through grade 1 for Step 1, grades 1 through 3 for Step 2, grades 2 and 3 for Step 3, and grades 2 through 4 for Step 4—are intended only as guides. Some children move through all four steps very rapidly; others climb the steps over a period of several years. These books will help your child "step into reading" in style!

*To Sam, Rachel, and Sarah*
—J.M.

*To Babe*
—B.S.

*Library of Congress Cataloging-in-Publication Data:* Marzollo, Jean. Soccer Sam. (Step into reading. A Step 3 book) SUMMARY: Sam's cousin from Mexico comes for an extended visit and teaches Sam and all the second graders to play soccer. [1. Soccer—Fiction. 2. Mexicans—United States—Fiction] I. Sims, Blanche, ill. II. Title. III. Series: Step into reading. Step 3 book.   PZ7.M3688So   1987 [E]   86-47533   ISBN: 0-394-88406-X (trade); 0-394-98406-4 (lib. bdg.)

Manufactured in the United States of America    22  23  24  25  26  27  28  29  30

STEP INTO READING is a trademark of Random House, Inc.

Step into Reading

# SOCCER SAM

by Jean Marzollo
illustrated by Blanche Sims

A Step 3 Book

Random House 🏠 New York

The plane from Mexico was landing.
Sam stood at the airport window
and watched. He was going to meet
his cousin Marco for the first time.

Soon a boy Sam's size came through
the door. Sam's mother hugged him.
"Marco, this is Sam," she said slowly.
"Sam, this is Marco."

"Hi," said Sam. Suddenly he felt shy.

"¡Hola!" said Marco softly.

In the car Marco was very quiet. So was Sam.

"We are happy you have come to live with us for a year," said Sam's mother.

"Sí," said Marco. But he didn't look happy. He just looked out the window.

"You like sports?" asked Sam. Sam loved sports. He was very good at them too.

Marco shrugged.

"He doesn't speak much English," said Sam's mother. When they got home, she said, "Take Marco out to play, Sam. Introduce him to your friends."

"What if he doesn't understand what we say?" asked Sam.

"Speak slowly," said his mom. "He'll learn."

Sam and Marco went outside. At the end of the street, kids were shooting baskets. Sam's friend Rosie tossed him the ball. Sam aimed and fired. The ball sailed through the rim.

"This is my cousin Marco," Sam said.
He tried to talk slowly, but it was hard.
"Marco, this is Billy, Chris, Rosie,
Tommy, and Freddy."

Billy shot Marco the ball. Marco caught it on his head and bounced it up and down like a seal. Everyone started to laugh at him. Sam's face got hot. He grabbed the ball and made another basket.

Chris caught the ball under the net. He threw it to Marco.

This time Marco caught the ball on his knee and bounced it up and down.

Again everyone laughed at him.

12

Sam felt awful. "Let's go home," he told Marco.

The next day Sam and Marco went to school together. At recess they played kickball. When the ball came to Marco, he stopped it with his feet.

"Don't you ever use your arms?" asked Freddy. But Marco didn't understand. The next time the ball came to him, he stopped it with his feet again.

Back home Sam tried to explain the rules of sports to Marco.

"Hold the ball in your hands," said Sam. "When you play basketball, bounce the ball as you run. It's called dribbling."

But Marco just looked at Sam. He didn't understand English. He couldn't even say Sam's name right. He said Sammee.

The next day after school, Sam didn't want to go outside. He didn't want to play ball. He was afraid his friends would make fun of Marco.

"Why don't you draw?" Sam's mother asked. So Sam got out his crayons. He drew a picture of a basketball player. Marco drew a picture of his mother and father.

Sam's mother looked at the pictures. "You know what I think?" she said. "I think Marco's homesick. Let's take him to the mall to cheer him up."

At the mall Sam's mother bought Marco a Giants shirt. But it didn't make Marco happy. He didn't know who the Giants were.

"Let's try some video games," said
Sam. "Watch. I'll show you how to play."
Sam played Pac-Man and got a very high
score. "Now you go," he said to Marco.
"Don't worry if you don't get a good
score at first."

Marco played Pac-Man and got a
better score than Sam. He laughed. "In
Mexico is Pac-Man also," he said. Marco
beat Sam at every game in the arcade.

They walked farther down the mall, looking at stores. When they came to the sports store, Sam stopped to look at footballs. But Marco wasn't interested in footballs. He ran over to a display of black and white balls in boxes. Suddenly he was grinning from ear to ear.

"Why didn't I think of this before?"
said Sam's mom. "Most kids in Mexico
play soccer."

"Soccer? Nobody plays that around
here," said Sam.

"Well, maybe they will now," said his
mother with a smile.

Back home Marco took his new ball outside. He bounced it on his head. He kicked it around with his feet.

Chris and Billy came over. Marco kicked the ball to Chris. Chris caught it with his hands.

"No hands," said Marco.

He kicked the ball to Billy. Billy caught it with his hands too.

"No hands!" yelled Marco. "Head! Head!" He bounced the ball on his head.

Then Marco kicked the ball to Sam.
Sam let the ball fall on his head.

"¡Bueno!" cried Marco. "¡Bueno,
Sammee!"

Sam laughed. He kicked the ball back
to Marco, who kicked it to Billy. Billy
bounced it back to Sam with his head.

"¡Bueno, Billy!" said Marco. Then he kicked the ball to Chris.

Chris caught it on his head and bounced it to Billy. Billy caught it on his head and bounced it to Sam.

"This is awesome!" said Sam.

"Let's bring the ball to school tomorrow," said Chris.

"We'll show the other kids how to play," said Billy.

"¡Bueno!" said Marco. "Good!"

The next day at recess Marco showed the other second graders how to play soccer. They stood in a circle and passed the ball around with their heads. Once Sam caught the ball with his hands.

"No hands!" yelled Marco.

The next time someone caught the ball with his hands, everyone yelled, "NO HANDS!" It was fun.

Then Marco told them to pass the ball with their feet. Once Chris picked up the ball with his hands. "NO HANDS!" everyone shouted.

The third graders came by and laughed. "No hands?" they said. "What a weird game."

Some of the second graders felt stupid. They didn't like to be teased by third graders.

"Forget it," said Sam. "I've got
a plan. Let's practice all week. Then
we'll challenge the third graders to
a game. They beat us in football. They
beat us in basketball. And they beat us
in baseball. But they won't beat us
in soccer, will they?"

The second graders liked the plan.
They practiced all week. Sam practiced
most of all.

On Friday morning Sam went up to the third graders in the playground. "If you think you're so hot," he said, "play soccer with us at lunch. Then we'll see who's really hot."

The third graders took the challenge. Then everyone went back to class. It was hard to study.

Billy said 5 plus 4 was 8.

Chris dropped his notebook on the floor and all his papers fell out.

Marco was so excited
he forgot the capital
of the United States.
He said it was
Dallas, Texas.

Sam was so excited, he could hardly write his spelling words.

Finally it was lunchtime. Everyone ate quickly and rushed outside.

The second and third graders met on the field. Sam marked the goals with jackets. Billy went over the rules. "Only the goalie can catch the ball," he said. "To score you have to kick the ball past the goalie and into the place marked by jackets."

The game began. Marco passed the ball to Chris. Chris started to dribble the ball up the field. One of the third graders ran in front of him. Chris passed the ball to Sam.

Sam kicked the ball hard but missed.
The ball sat on the field. A third grader
ran up and kicked it way down the field.

What a kick! The third graders were really big and strong. Another third grader kicked the ball into the third graders' goal. The score was 1–0. The third graders were ahead.

Sam looked worried.

"No problema," said Marco. He
dribbled the ball to the opposite goal all
by himself. Third graders tried to get the
ball away from Marco, but he zigzagged
around them. Two of the third graders
fell down trying to catch Marco.

"Go, Marco baby!" yelled Billy.

Marco kicked the ball at the second graders' goal. It went in! Now the score was a 1–1 tie.

"Hooray!" shouted Sam.

The third graders had the ball now. One of them kicked it halfway down the field. Another one dribbled it to the third-grade goal. He took aim and fired. Tommy, who was goalie for the second graders, caught the ball.

"Hooray!" shouted Sam again. He knew it was all right for Tommy to catch the ball. In soccer, goalies are the only players who can do that.

Freddy threw the ball to Sam. Sam passed it to Marco. Marco ran it down to the other end and passed it back to Sam. Sam gave it a good hard kick. The ball sailed over the goalie's head. Now the score was 2–1.

The third graders weren't used to
losing. They began to make mistakes.
They caught the ball with their hands.
Every time they did, the second graders
shouted, "NO HANDS!"

The second graders started scoring like crazy. Bam! Chris got a goal. Slam! He got another one. Wham! Wham! Wham! Billy got one goal, and Rosie got two.

But Sam and Marco were the team stars. They ran circles around the third graders. They scored six goals each. When lunchtime was over, the score was 19–1.

"A wipe-out!" said Sam.

The third graders were good losers.
They all shook hands with the
second graders. Then they asked Marco
if he would teach them how to play
better.

"Sí," said Marco. "Soccer Sammee teach you too."

Everybody laughed. "Soccer Sammee!" they shouted. "Soccer Sammee!"

And that's how Sam got his nickname. At first he wasn't sure if he liked it or not.

"Is bueno?" asked Marco. "You like new name?"

Sam looked at his cousin. He knew that anything Marco gave him, he would like. "Sí," said Sam. "I like. Gracias."